W9-ATG-723

Totally Twins

Model Mania

The Fabulous Diary of
Persephone Pinchgut

To my family.
— Aleesah Darlison

For Tanya, Moni and Di.
Finally, someone wrote a book about
the four of us!
— Serena Geddes

American edition published in 2021
by New Frontier Publishing Europe Ltd
www.newfrontierpublishing.us
First published in Australia in 2010 by
New Frontier Publishing Pty Ltd
ABN 67 126 171 757

Suite 83/20-40 Meagher Street, Chippendale NSW 2008

www.newfrontier.com.au

ISBN: 978-1-913639-37-2

Distributed in the United States and Canada by Lerner Publishing Group Inc
241 First Avenue North, Minneapolis, MN 55401 USA
www.lernerbooks.com

Library of Congress Cataloging-in-Publication data is available
Designed by Celeste Hulme and Nicholas Pike
Printed in China
1 3 5 7 9 10 8 6 4 2

Totally Twins

Model Mania

The Fabulous Diary of
Persephone Pinchgut

Aleesah Darlison
Illustrated by Serena Geddes

NEW FRONTIER PUBLISHING

Sunday, March 21, 7:43 a.m.

Cozy in bed.

Yes, I know it's Sunday morning and impossibly early, but I can't sleep. I bought this new diary yesterday and I've been dying to write in it. So many fresh pages to fill!

So here's the scoop. I'm Persephone River Pinchgut and this is my second ever personal diary. My first diary started out *TOP SECRET* because I didn't want my twin sister, Portia, snooping. She eventually found out about it anyway—but promised not to snoop—so my diarizing is now out in the open.

Portia and I are identical twins. We're in Fifth Grade at Heartfield Heights Elementary School. We're ten: very nearly eleven. I'd like

to think I'm the more mature and sensible twin, but Portia would probably say that I'm just too serious and a worrywart.

We live with our mom, Skye, who is into weird and unusual things. When she was pregnant with Portia and me, she was into Greek mythology and Shakespeare. That's why she named me after the Goddess of the Underworld and Portia after the heroine in that old bearded guy's (Shakespeare's) play, *The Merchant of Venice.*

At the moment, Mom is into yoga and laughter therapy. She teaches classes for both out of our living room. Usually we have lots of people over here stretching and groaning, "ommming" and "ahhhhing," or giggling their heads off. Strange, I know, but that's the way it is.

Our dad, Pickford, moved to England two years ago after he split up with Mom. He's remarried. His new wife is Eleanor Elizabeth Krankston. Her initials are *E.E.K.* so Portia and I call her *EEK!* (Teehee)

My gran, who visits sometimes, travels a lot because she's a travel writer. She is totally cool. She bungee jumps, cycles, and swims in the ocean. Even in winter. Brrr!

As for Portia—my evil twin (only joking!)—she obviously looks like me because we're identical. Same yellow hair, same crystal-green "cat's eyes," as Mom calls them, same pointy elbows, and skinny fingers. The only difference is that I have a teardrop-shaped mole on my left cheek and Portia doesn't. I call it a beauty spot. Portia calls it a smudge. I think she's jealous because she wants a beauty spot of her own.

Portia is so into girly things, like ballet and fashion, and anything pink or glittery. I prefer Egyptian archaeology, swimming, reading, and diary writing. See, I am more sensible.

Portia always wears her hair out and flicks it around everywhere. I wear my hair in a ponytail with four bobby pins on either side so nothing escapes. I like my hair tidy because I'm a neat person. Portia likes her hair "flowing," as

she calls it. I think that's because she's a rather messy person. If you could see our room right now (we have to share) you'd see it's true.

So even though Portia and I look the same, we think differently. Often that leads to problems.

FIVE FABULOUS THINGS YOU NEED TO KNOW ABOUT ME

1. My birthday is May 29.
2. My star sign is Gemini: the twins. Spooky coincidence or what?
3. My favorite color is purple.
4. My secret ambition is to learn to surf.
5. My secret fear is SHARKS (because of a movie I once saw), so achieving my secret ambition in point four may take a while!

Sunday, March 21, 1:57 p.m.

On the back porch, soaking up the sun.

I'm totally full! I have just finished lunch (creamy pumpkin risotto), which was *YUMMY*. Mr. Divine came over; Mom always tries to impress him with her cooking. Although she's a vegetarian, she does have a good repertoire of excellent meals. When she doesn't burn them, that is.

BTW (by the way), Mr. Divine is Mom's art teacher from college (she's into *ABSTRACT* painting). Ever since Mr. Divine helped Mom with her art exhibition—which was a huge success—they have been spending time together. One day they might become boyfriend and girlfriend, but for now they're "taking things

slowly." Whatever that means.

Mr. Divine is kind and handsome, even for an elderly person of thirty-something. He's tall with sparkly, green eyes, springy, brown hair, and a goatee.

While I don't mind Mr. Divine, Portia doesn't like him at all. She can't help herself and mentions Dad every time Mr. Divine is around. I suspect he knows Portia doesn't like him because he brought a fashion magazine over

for her today to "butter her up," as Gran would say. He brought a book on Ancient Egypt for me. He doesn't need to butter me up though. As long as he's nice to Mom, I'm happy.

I didn't have the heart to tell Mr. Divine I already had the Egyptian book. Mom knew I did though, and shot me a look that said, "Please don't say anything." So I smiled and said, "Thanks. I love books on Ancient Egypt," which earned me a secret wink from Mom. Cool!

Despite how she feels about Mr. Divine, Portia loved the magazine he gave her. When she spotted this advertisement for a modeling agency in it, she asked Mom if she could register with them, because apparently all she's ever wanted was to be a model. At least this week anyway.

Mom frowned and said she was sure there

was something more worthwhile Portia could aspire to, like being a doctor or a social worker. Portia rolled her eyes and snorted.

"That is so not what I want to be," she told Mom. "I won't get rich or famous if I'm a doctor or social worker."

Then she practically begged Mom to call the modeling agency, saying, "Pretty please!" over and over.

"We'll see," Mom relented, after a while.

Portia and I knew she'd won. A "we'll see" from Mom means it's only a matter of time before it's a "yes."

Knowing precisely when to quit, Portia flashed me a SECRET SIGNAL that said "Told you so," then flounced out of the room.

FIVE THINGS I WOULD DO IF I WAS RICH AND FAMOUS

1. Have foot massages every day.
2. Hire a housekeeper to tidy up after Mom and Portia so I'd never have to trip over their mess again.
3. Make Dad visit more often by picking him up in my private jet. I'd even let EEK! come.
4. Buy a super-sized tub of honeycomb crunch ice cream with colorful sprinkles on top: EVERY DAY. Then eat the lot.
5. Build my own house (Mom and Portia could still live with me) in the shape of an Egyptian pyramid. How cool would that be?

Sunday, March 21, 9:32 p.m.

Tucked up in bed.

Latest update on the wanna-be-a-model saga: victory to Portia! She's talked Mom into making an appointment with the modeling agency. Mom's going to call tomorrow while we're at school.

Portia is on her bed snoring as I write this. The magazine Mr. Divine brought over is covering her face because she fell asleep reading it. I've got school tomorrow, so I'd better turn out the light before Mom comes in to check on me. *TTYL* (talk to you later.)

Monday, March 22. 4:43 p.m.

In the kitchen.

I’m munching on one of Mom’s butterscotch muffins as I write. Mom isn’t here because she’s at her college art course. Portia and I are “fending for ourselves,” as Gran would say. We don’t mind. We’re used to it.

Mom left us a note on the fridge:

Hi girls,
Muffins on table. Enjoy! Modeling agency appointment at 4p.m. tomorrow. See you at 6.
Love, Mom XX

Usually Portia stuffs her face with Mom’s muffins. Not today. She didn’t want any because

apparently she has to stay in shape for her modeling.

I waved a muffin under her nose and asked, "What modeling?" and Portia said, "You'll see," then skipped down the hall to our room. Guess that means more muffins for me.

Portia asked me to go with her to the agency tomorrow. I told her I had better things to do with my time (like counting the number of entries under B in the dictionary), but she said I had to go because I was her sister and she needed my support. I suppose it might be interesting to see what happens.

Portia's so pumped! You should have heard her going on about it at school today.

"I'm gonna be famous," she said, before Jolie and Caitlin had even put their bags down. "A famous model, like in the magazines."

BTW, Jolie and Caitlin are Portia and my best friends. We're a neat gang of four. We hang out together all the time. This morning, when Portia broke the news, we were in our usual spot at the picnic table near the school's herb garden.

Caitlin and Jolie were totally impressed.

Caitlin asked, "Since when have you wanted to be a model?"

"Since Mom agreed to register me with the Heavenly Models Agency," Portia said. 'It's only a matter of time before I'm so famous that you'll be seeing my face everywhere."

I know my sister can be imaginative at times,

but I thought she was totally *DELUSIONAL* so I joked that I already see her face everywhere because it's the same as mine. Portia didn't think that was funny at all and stuck her nose in the air and said, "Actually, I'm already famous. I've been in the newspaper lots of times." I thought it was my duty to remind her she'd only been in the paper once. Portia sniffed and said, "Oh yeah, that's right," like she'd forgotten.

I also reminded her that it was ages ago that we won the Beautiful Babies Competition and that she couldn't keep trading off her baby stardom forever. Plus, being in the paper *ONCE* didn't make her famous. It's not like I'm using it as a fame ticket, so why should she?

That's when Portia mumbled that even supermodels had to start somewhere. Then the bell rang so we had to go into class. That

didn't stop Portia talking about her upcoming modeling career, though. She kept going on about it all day!

Boy, I hope this works out. Portia will be totally *SHATTERED* if it doesn't.

Monday, March 22, 7:24 p.m.

Lounging on my bed.

Mom arrived home a while ago. She was late as usual, but I've forgiven her because she brought a takeout with her (A RARE EVENT). Admittedly, it was from the organic salad shop so it was ultra-healthy and possibly something a rabbit would eat, but it was tasty.

While we were nibbling our rabbit food, Mom told us Mr. Divine had asked her out on a date.

"I know I've only known Will a few months, but it's taken me a long time since your father left to:

a) feel like dating again

b) actually find someone I like."

And yes, she did talk in point form.

I heard Portia make a low, rumbling growl in her throat: like a dog guarding a bone.

Mom tucked her hair behind her ear (she's usually fibbing when she does that) and hurried on, saying Mr. Divine had asked her to a play this Saturday night and she'd said yes. She said if we didn't want her to go, she'd call it off.

I told her I was okay with it and, honestly, I wasn't trying to earn brownie points. It was the truth. Like I said, I like Mr. Divine and I want Mom to be happy. She deserves to be happy because she's worked hard and looked after us on her own since Dad left.

Portia didn't think the same way though. She said she thought Mom and Mr. Divine were just friends and that friends didn't date: at least not each other. Mom agreed that they were friends, but they now wanted to take their relationship to the next level. Whatever that means.

Portia opened her mouth to protest, but I shot her a SECRET SIGNAL, well several actually, that said, "Give it a rest," "Don't be so hard on her," and, with a flick of my eyes at the note on the fridge, "Remember your modeling interview." Which sounds complicated, but because Portia and I know each other so well the message got through.

Portia nodded, then mumbled that she was sorry and, of course, Mom could go out with Mr. Divine. Mom beamed as she hugged us, which made me realize we'd done the right

thing. Then came the bombshell.

"The play starts at seven, so Will's picking me up at six-thirty," Mom said. "Mrs. Pickleton will bring dinner, and Dill, when she comes over."

Mrs. Pickleton is our next-door neighbor and Mom's biggest yoga fan. Her clothes are always ultra-bright and ultra-busy (usually with floral or animal prints) and her fuchsia-colored hair has purple streaks in it. Weird. She is, however, a terrific seamstress. She made our costumes for the class musical recently.

The only problem is that her seven-year-old son, Dillon (or Dill Pickle as Portia and I call him), is totally fascinated with Portia and me and

our *IDENTICAL-NESS*. He can never tell us apart and always asks silly twin-related questions.

Portia and I insisted we were old enough to look after ourselves at night because we do it enough in the afternoons. Mom wouldn't listen. She said anything could happen and she'd feel better if Mrs. Pickleton was with us.

We even asked whether Gran could mind us instead, but Mom said Gran was flying to Barbados on Sunday morning so she had to get an early night. Then she said it was all settled with Mrs. Pickleton anyway and that was that.

Tuesday, March 23, 4:34 p.m.

Heavenly Models Agency.

I knew there would be a lot of waiting around at the agency with Portia, so I brought my diary. I was right too; the agent is already fifteen minutes late.

Mom, Portia, and I are in the reception area. Its stark, white walls are covered with black-and-white photos of famous people. The receptionist asked Portia to fill in a form while we wait. It asks ultra-personal questions like her height and weight and whether she has any previous modeling experience.

Portia wrote down the Beautiful Babies

Competition, but I told her that was ridiculous, so she rubbed it out.

Here we go! The agent's here.

Tuesday, March 23, 5:08 p.m.

Heavenly Models Agency continued...

The agent's name is Hilary Bonaparte and she's wearing the tallest high heels *EVER*. She's also wearing bright, pink lipstick and her perfume is so strong it's making me sneeze. Worse than that, she didn't even apologize for being late!

When Hilary finally ushered us into her room she stared at Portia and me for a minute, her eyes flicking back and forth before she asked if we were twins. Portia said yes and Hilary said that was fabulous because she wanted twins on her books and we would be so cute together. Blurh!

Before I could reply, Portia sorted Hilary out

by telling her I wasn't interested in modeling. She's got that right!

Hilary did an *ARE-YOU-CRAZY?* eyebrow lift at me, then said it was a shame, but all right. She talked at a million miles an hour about what modeling was like and the jobs Portia might be asked to do.

Then Hilary said Portia needed photographs taken for her portfolio. She also mentioned it would cost a hundred and fifty dollars, but that Portia would soon make her money back when she started working. Portia glanced at Mom for approval.

“We’re here now so we may as well get them done,” Mom sighed.

Now I’m sitting at the back of the studio while Portia has her photos taken. She keeps having to change outfits and props and positions and the flash keeps going *POP! POP! POP!* I think I’m getting a headache.

Tuesday, March 23, 8:57 p.m.

In my bedroom.

It took *FOREVER* at the agency this afternoon. I don't know what Portia sees in this modeling thing. It's totally tedious if you ask me.

When we got home, Portia got straight on the internet to research deportment and grooming courses. You know, where you walk around balancing a book on your head. Apparently this sort of thing makes you walk properly: straight and upright.

She printed out the details of one she liked and I've stuck it in here:

Deportment and Grooming

is the first step for any professional model.

Awaken your inner princess!

Our courses will:

- ★ Build your confidence
- ★ Improve your image, style, and posture
- ★ Teach you makeup techniques to highlight your best features
- ★ Polish your manners and conversational skills
- ★ Improve speech and breath control

Now all Portia has to do is convince Mom to pay the money to "awaken her inner princess"!

Thursday, March 25, 8:02 a.m.

In the kitchen, munching fruit salad for breakfast.

Portia's photos arrived this morning by courier. She's been staring at them ever since and seems totally *IN LOVE* with her own image.

Mom's whizzing about the house, throwing clothes in the washing machine and tidying up *(TWO RARE EVENTS).* To earn extra money, she's started a new meditation class on Thursday nights. She has to tidy up this morning because she'll be in the city all day running a laughter therapy workshop and won't get a chance to do it before her meditation session tonight. Mom's hardly had time to glance at Portia's photos, which Portia is not happy about.

I looked at the photos after prising them away

from Portia. They're *FABULOUS*. They are all very glamorous. Very model-like. Very Portia.

It's strange seeing your sister (and in a way, almost yourself) looking so grown-up. A teeny-tiny part of me wishes I'd had my photos taken too. But a bigger part of me, the part that definitely doesn't want to do modeling because I would be way too nervous, knows I've made the right decision. This is Portia's thing, not mine.

Portia asked Mom if she could take the photos to school. For some reason (probably because she's flat-out) Mom said yes. Portia only had to ask once!

Mom's now dashing out the door. She left a wet kiss on my cheek as she went. I'd better go too. I still have to brush my teeth and hair.

Hey! Mom dropped her laughter therapy tip sheet on her way out. I've pasted it in here to give you a giggle.

FIVE FUN TIPS FROM SKYE

1. List all the things that make you laugh
2. Thumb wrestle with someone
3. Blow raspberries when you feel like it
4. Draw a funny picture of yourself, then show others
5. Give someone a hug

Thursday, March 25, 3:52 p.m.

Lounging in the living room.

First thing this morning at school, Portia shoved her photos at Caitlin and Jolie and warned them to be careful not to mark them otherwise Mom would freak out.

Once Jolie and Caitlin had looked at the photos and said how great they were, Portia took them back and sat at the picnic table going through them again and again.

Caitlin handed Jolie and me matching yellow envelopes with shiny star stickers on them. She told us they were our invitations to the "Party of the Year." She also gave Portia one, but Portia was too busy admiring her photos to read it. Caitlin saw that Portia ignored it, but didn't say anything.

Anyway, Jolie, Caitlin, and I went into a group huddle and read out the invitations.

Of course, Jolie and I said "Yes!" instantly. As if we would miss our friend's birthday party!

You won't believe this—Portia's been offered her first modeling assignment! Hilary Bonaparte just phoned to say there's a fashion parade at the mall on Saturday and one of the boutiques needs a girl Portia's age and size to model their clothes, and did she want the job?

As soon as Portia stopped squealing and jumping up and down, she said, "Yes!" So this is it. Portia's modeling career has officially commenced.

Hang on, Mom's home. I want to hear Portia tell her all about this before the onslaught of the meditation people.

Thursday, March 25, 7:44 p.m.

Barricaded in our room.

"KEEP OUT"

Mom came home *GLOWING* after her laughter therapy session in the city. She was so excited and said it went very well. Who would have thought that grown-ups needed to be taught how to laugh? Still, there may be more to Mom's glowing than just a good session. I can't put my finger on what it is though.

There are ridiculous sounds coming from the living room right now. Mom's in the middle of her meditation session and the "ommming" and "ahhhhing" echoing around the house is rather disturbing. How can people relax with all that noise?

Portia and I are in our bedroom. We're meant to be doing our homework, but we can't concentrate because we're giggling too much at the odd sounds. Plus, the smell of incense (sandalwood) that Mom insists on burning during her sessions is enough to put anyone off math. Not that I need an excuse.

Although I'm giggling with Portia, truth be told I'm a bit mad at her. I understand that she's ecstatic about this fashion parade (which Mom said she could do, *BTW*) but she's forgetting her friends, or at least one of them. She hurt Caitlin's feelings today by ignoring her invitation. It took her until lunch break to remember she even

had it because she was so busy being *POSSIBLY-FAMOUS*. Even then, I had to remind her.

We were sitting on the jungle gym where we sometimes hang out so we can spy on other kids (and teachers) in the playground. I was munching a cheese and lettuce sandwich on whole grain (my favorite) and I tugged Portia's foot and asked in a whisper if she was going to mention anything about Caitlin's party.

She asked, "What party?"

"The party you got an invitation to this morning," I said. "Remember?"

Portia's brain suddenly clicked into gear. You could practically see it working behind her eyes. She tugged the crumpled invitation out of her pocket, scratching her chin as she read it.

"What's up?" Caitlin asked, noticing Portia reading her invitation.

"Nothing," Portia said. "Sounds cool, it's just—"

"Just what?" Caitlin said.

Portia shrugged. "It's nothing really. It's just that I've heard about these awesome model-for-a-day catwalk parties that sound way more grown-up than a roller-skating party."

How rude!

Caitlin froze, staring at Portia with her mouth open like one of those grouper fish.

Tension fizzed in the air. No one knew what to say, so we didn't say anything. After that, Portia and Caitlin didn't talk for the rest of the day, which isn't like them at all because they're always gabbing on together.

I'll finish writing now because the meditators have gone and *River's Town*, my favorite of favorite TV shows, is about to start. The main character in the show is called River (same as my middle name; how cool is that?) and she's played by an actress called Taylor North. Taylor North is SOOOOO good-looking and cool, and she's such a great actress. River is fourteen and the daughter of a wealthy lawyer in a small town. Far from being snobbish though, she's friendly and kind. I'm sure Taylor North must be just like River in real life. The role seems to come so naturally to her.

Must dash!

Portia spilled the beans about the mall fashion parade at school today.

"I got my first modeling assignment!" she told Caitlin and Jolie. "I'm going to be in a fashion parade at the mall tomorrow."

Caitlin didn't say anything (I think she was still cross about Portia's behavior the day before), but Jolie asked what time it was. Portia was getting ready for a huge rabbiting-on when Flynn MacIntosh (who is rather cute, but I'd never tell him that) wandered over. He showed us a photo of three tiny kittens. Flynn was trying to find good homes for them, because his dad

said he couldn't keep them.

I remembered a few weeks ago Flynn asking me if I liked kittens. Unfortunately, he thought I was Portia at the time. Just before that, he'd sent Portia a Valentine's Day card with a kitten on the front. At least, I think he sent the card. It wasn't signed, but I was sure Flynn liked Portia because I'd caught him staring at her. Maybe I was wrong. Maybe Flynn had been asking me about kittens because he had some to give away, not because he'd bought a kitten card. But if Flynn didn't give Portia the card, who did?

Anyway, Jolie said she'd ask her mom if she could have a kitten. Caitlin said she liked the orange one, but she wouldn't be able to get it. Her dog, Caesar, is a Rottweiler and would probably eat it for breakfast.

I would have *LOVED* a kitten, but I know Mom

and Portia are less than keen on animals. They think they're messy and *HIGH MAINTENANCE*. They're fine ones to talk!

When Flynn wandered off, Portia immediately steered the conversation back to her modeling. She said she would probably be super-nervous, but it would be great if Jolie and Caitlin could come and watch. Jolie said she'd come for sure, but Caitlin said she had to watch her brothers (she has three) play soccer.

Portia was *MIFFED* by that. We all know Caitlin can't stand soccer and gets dragged along to

watch the games. Usually she tries to get out of it, but apparently not this weekend.

The bell rang and we lined up to go into class, all the while chatting about the fashion parade. Hayley and Charlotte, two girls in our class, overheard us talking and asked Portia if she was a model.

Of course, Portia said yes and told them all about her burgeoning modeling career, her agent and the upcoming fashion parade. I saw Caitlin roll her eyes. After that she went dead quiet.

Hayley and Charlotte started gushing and saying things like, "Wow!" and, "That's so exciting!" I pinched Portia's arm and sent her a SECRET SIGNAL of "Get over yourself," but she shook me off.

I know Portia's excited, but she needs to tone

it down. She's getting ahead of herself with this modeling.

BTW, I sure hope it's not the end of her friendship with Caitlin.

Saturday, March 27, 9:37 a.m.

Crammed into a portable dressing room.

We've been at the mall since nine, with Portia trying on all sorts of clothes for this boutique she's modeling for. Of course, she roped me into coming. Mom said she would have loved to come but, as usual, she had a laughter therapy session she couldn't get out of. I'm missing swimming for this, but Portia is oblivious to my sacrifice. All she said was, "It won't kill you to miss swimming this once."

I knew I'd be waiting around a lot while Portia swanned about, so I brought my diary so I could stay busy.

The stage in the food court is decked out

with a runway for the models to strut along. A guy is checking the sound system, tapping the microphone, and giving loud blasts of music every so often to make sure it's working.

The music will have to be *BLARING* to be heard over the rain which is hammering on the glass ceiling. There are puddles forming everywhere and cold currents of air are slicing through the place. The mall is quite "open to the elements," as Gran would say. Somehow, I don't think Caitlin

will be watching her brothers play soccer today. I wonder if she'll come here instead?

Portia's "dressing room" is actually a metal frame with flimsy white curtains sewn onto it that are flapping like crazy in the breeze. It will be a miracle if Portia doesn't give the crowd a *SNEAK PREVIEW* of her underwear while she's changing costumes!

Thirteen girls, besides Portia, are modeling outfits for the various shops.

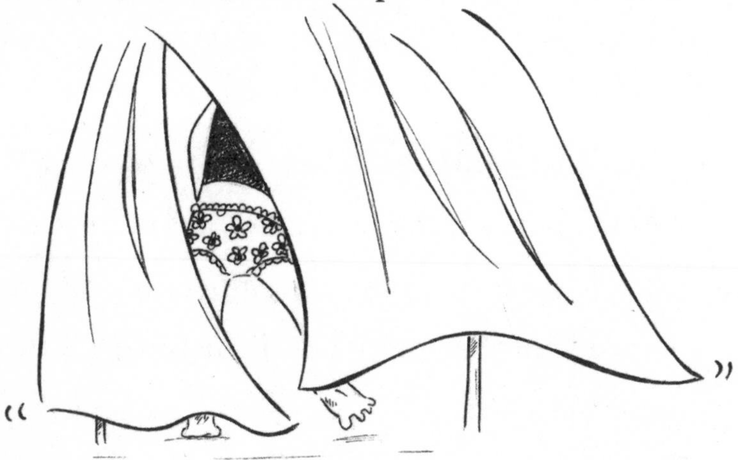

Most of them are way older than her. The only other girl Portia's age is Mischa, whose mom owns the shop she and Portia are modeling for, called, *Sadie's Funky Fashion Boutique*. Mischa is pretty, with long, straight, black hair, dark eyes, olive skin, and a delicate, pointy nose. When Portia asked her if she was a model, Mischa laughed and said no, she was too short and that she did the fashion parade to help her mom out.

Peeking through the curtains of the dressing room, I saw that the white plastic chairs lined up out the front of the stage were already filling up. I guess when it's TORRENTIAL outside people can't do much but go to the mall.

I asked Mischa if she ever got nervous. She shook her head and said she was used to it, that it was just a bit of fun. Unfortunately, Portia

wasn't used to it. Her hands were shaking and she was as pale as the flippy-flappy dressing room curtains.

Mom says calming your breath calms your mind. It's worked for me before, so I told Portia to practice her ujjayi breathing like Mom does in yoga. I held Portia's hands and together we breathed in and out. Slow. Deep. Rhythmic.

Haaaa… Haaaa…

"It's just a bit of fun," Portia chanted between breaths. "It's just a bit of fun."

Saturday, March 27, 12:49 p.m.

Still at the mall, waiting for Mom to pick us up.

What's keeping Mom? She promised to pick us up at twelve-thirty, but she's still not here. That woman is always late! We're waiting in the mall car park. Portia is practicing her runway walk.

I have to say, Portia did a great job modeling Sadie's funky fashions. She didn't trip once or make an idiot of herself like we both thought she would. She looked so poised and confident on the runway I had to do a double take to make sure it was Portia. She'd been so nervous before. Looks like it was only stage fright.

Jolie arrived as the parade started. She

slipped into a chair beside me and we watched as the models took turns going down the runway. When the announcer said, "And now from *Sadie's Funky Fashion Boutique,* we have Mischa Ward and Portia Pinchgut!" Jolie and I clapped and cheered loudly. I looked around for Caitlin, but there was no sign of her.

Portia glided elegantly down the runway toward us. I don't know where she learned to walk like that, but she looked so professional: head high; back straight; smiling. Then she turned and SASHAYED back up the catwalk after Mischa, as if she'd been modeling for years.

When the parade was over, Jolie and I congratulated Portia and told her how fabulous she was. Mischa and her mom, Sadie, agreed. Portia was even allowed to keep one of the outfits she'd modeled as a special thank-you.

But that's not all.

A guy in a business suit came up and introduced himself to Portia.

"I'm Lex Gable," he said. "I own this shopping center and I saw you on the runway. You were great out there!"

Portia blushed and thanked him. Then he

asked her if she was interested in more work. Apparently, the shopping center catalog is coming out next week, but one of their models had to pull out of the photo shoot because she has chicken pox. Lex said Portia would be perfect for the job and asked if she wanted it.

Portia said she was very interested, but that Lex would have to speak to her agent. She handed him one of Hilary's business cards, all the while looking and sounding totally cool and calm. Jolie and I could only watch and learn from "The Master."

When Portia asked when the photo shoot was, Lex said it was Tuesday, which he realized was a bit of a rush, but he had a deadline to get the catalog into people's mailboxes before Friday. I reminded Portia that Tuesday was a school day, but she rolled her eyes and said it would be fine to skip it this once. I only hope for her sake Mom agrees.

After Lex left, Portia, Jolie, and I had a group giggle. Jolie and I were both so excited for Portia and said we couldn't believe how quickly things were happening for her.

Portia didn't seem fazed at all though and said, "That's fame for you, I suppose."

Finally! Mom's here. Boy, is she in trouble for being late.

Saturday, March 27, 5:41 p.m.

Sitting at my desk.

Unbelievably, Mom agreed Portia could do the photo shoot on Tuesday. She's even agreed to take her.

But that's not all.

Apart from Portia's stunning success at the fashion parade, it seems Mom has struck gold with her laughter therapy workshops. When we got home from the mall, a silver Mercedes was parked in our driveway, blocking it completely so that Mom had to park in the street. As we walked up the path to the front door, a huge man stepped out of the huge Merc.

At first Mom was blinking a lot, like she was in shock. I even saw her lip tremble slightly.

Then she smiled and shook the man's hand. He was so big his hand swallowed Mom's! He was wearing a blue collared shirt, jeans, and black polished shoes (not sneakers, even though it's the weekend) and his silver-streaked hair was gelled and combed back. All in all, he was neat and *EXPENSIVE-LOOKING*, not at all like Mr. Divine who is natural and *ARTISTIC-LOOKING*, but still handsome in his own way.

The Silver Man said something to Mom I didn't hear. All I saw was her blushing, like a little kid. Not sure what to do, I hung back but Portia marched over and introduced herself, then flung a hand at me and said I was her twin sister, Persephone.

The Silver Man smiled and said hello. I said "Hi," and quickly looked away from his dazzling, blue eyes because he was staring at me like he could read my thoughts.

Mom introduced him, saying, "Girls, this is Morcum Maximus. I did a laughter therapy workshop for his company on Thursday."

"And it's been a revelation for my staff," Morcum said, watching Mom as he spoke. "That's why I dropped by to speak to you, Skye. I hope you don't mind."

Mom blushed again and said she didn't mind

at all and invited Mr. Maximus inside. While Portia and I sat at the table sneaking stares at him, Mom hurried about the kitchen making herbal teas (chamomile, because it calms her nerves) and setting out slices of carrot cake on a plate. She also sent Portia and me a few SECRET SIGNALS of "Scram!" but we pretended not to notice. This was too good to miss!

Mr. Maximus asked Mom loads of questions about her alternative therapies business—and a few personal ones too. Then he told Mom he wanted her to run laughter workshops at all of his offices.

Most were near where we lived, but a few were in other states. When he asked Mom if she was willing to travel, she glanced at Portia and me and said she would need to think about it.

"Don't take too long," Mr. Maximus said. "I need you, Skye."

As he spoke he stood up and took Mom's hands in his and looked deeply into her eyes while she chewed her bottom lip. He seemed to be trying to tell her something without actually speaking. It was an intense moment, but over quickly so I can't be totally sure of what happened. Who knows what goes on with adults?

After Mr. Maximus left, we talked for ages about what would be involved. Portia and I agreed Mom should give it a go. She said she would try to travel during the week while we were at school so we wouldn't miss her and so

her yoga and painting wouldn't suffer. She said Gran might be able to mind us sometimes (when she's in the country) and that Mrs. Pickleton would probably help too.

I wasn't keen on the Pickleton option, but Mom was so excited and hopeful I didn't want to complain. This job meant extra money, and with Dad never sending any home I knew Mom struggled to get by some weeks.

When I asked Mom what Mr. Divine would think, her eyes bulged.

"Oh my goodness!" she gasped. "I forgot about our date."

Then she dashed into the bathroom, slamming the door behind her. She's still in there now, blow-drying her hair.

Sunday, March 28, 10:09 a.m.

After breakfast, sitting at my desk.

Here's the scoop on what happened last night on "the very important date."

Mom looked beautiful in a blue dress. Mr. Divine arrived to take her to the play, wearing tailored pants and a red-collared shirt. His goatee was neatly trimmed and his aftershave smelled of citrus. He even gave Mom a bunch of sweet-scented freesias (that's what Mrs. Pickleton said they were.) How romantic!

I think I heard Mom and Mr. Divine kiss, but I can't be sure because Mrs. Pickleton was dragging me into the kitchen at the time. Portia tried a last minute I-think-I'm-getting-a-headache routine, but it didn't work and Mom left.

While she was out, Portia and I were subjected to four hours of Dill Pickle's weird twin questions. Plus, we had to watch a boring old movie about a dog and a cat that get lost in the wild and have to find their way home. So predictable! Apparently, it's Dill's favorite movie, which he mentioned about seven thousand times.

Dill also ate about seven thousand honey sandwiches while he was over here. He's addicted to them if you ask me. Even after I told him the TRUE FACT that honey is really bee vomit, it didn't turn him off. Weird or what?

Dill continued his fascination with twins and insisted on asking ridiculous questions.

FIVE ANNOYING TWIN QUESTIONS DILL ASKED LAST NIGHT

1. Why don't you wear the same clothes?
2. Which one of you is better at tying shoelaces?
3. If one of you stubs your toe, does the other one feel it?
4. Do you ever play tricks on people and pretend you're the other one?
5. Do twins have superpowers?

The only interesting thing that happened was Gran phoning to say goodbye before heading off to Barbados. She said she was hoping to go to Fiji next school vacation and she might *TAKE PORTIA AND ME WITH HER!* Can you believe it? She said she wasn't sure yet and that she would have to see, but I hope, hope, *HOPE* it comes off. Fiji next vacation would be so cool!

I won't bore you with any more details of my ordinary night, except to say that Mom crept into the house super-late. She looks *EXCEEDINGLY* happy this morning with a smile as wide as the Grand Canyon. Since she got up she's been doing an abstract painting in red and yellow. I think that's a good sign for how things went last night.

Monday, March 29, 5:54 p.m.

My bedroom.

I can't believe it! I beat Portia in a math quiz today. She's so in a world of her own with her *MODELING* that she can't focus in class. Normally she hates me beating her in anything, especially math, but today she didn't even notice.

But that's not all.

Portia is so convinced she's now a fully-fledged model she's calling everyone "darling." She even said it to Miss Tamarind, our drama teacher, who nearly fell off her chair at the time. Portia's so preoccupied she didn't even realize she did it!

When Portia isn't calling people "darling" she's practicing her runway walk, loping around

the school tall and straight-backed. She also talks like she has a boiled candy in her mouth, all civilized and English-like. I'm sure Dad and *EEK!* would like it, but I think she sounds funny.

Hang on. Portia just walked in and said she has something important to show me. *TTYL*.

Monday, March 29, 6:15 p.m.

Still in my room.

Portia has disappeared to go watch some new modeling show on TV.

The important thing Portia had to show me was her "model pose." YAWN!

She said she learned it from a book she borrowed from the library. Mom said she couldn't do the *Deportment and Grooming/ Awaken Your Inner Princess Course* because it was too expensive. I guess the book was the next best thing.

When I told Portia she did an awesome snobby-person pose she said, "It's called modeling, darling. You know, like acting."

I told her it looked totally natural and that's

when she picked up her pillow and threw it at me, so I jumped up and whacked her with my pillow. It was fun having a giggle.

It's the photo shoot today and, for the first time in her life, Portia is up early. She's so chirpy and full of energy she's practically bouncing off the walls. I'm not happy though. I could have used another half hour of sleep.

Portia has already showered and is now brushing her hair so it shines. The latest news is that Mom won't be able to take Portia to the photo shoot after all. She got a call late last night from Mr. Maximus and he wants her to fly interstate today to do a laughter therapy workshop. I thought it was rude giving Mom practically no notice, but she said it was too good an opportunity to miss.

Instead of Mom going with Portia to the photo shoot, I have to. I suppose it's not so bad missing school for a day, but we were going to the aquarium, which isn't school-like at all, more like hanging out with your friends.

Portia doesn't mind that Mom isn't coming. She's just relieved she's still allowed to go. She enjoys showing off in front of me anyway. To keep boredom at bay, I'm taking plenty of snacks (seaweed rice crackers, bananas, and apricot cookies) and my diary. Must stop now; Portia's jumping on my bed to make me get up. Can't write!

Tuesday, March 30, 11:37 a.m.

Sitting in a corner of the room, out of the way.

We're in the photography studio now and there are cameras, lights, and white screens everywhere. I'm almost blinded from the flash and I'm not even the one having my photo taken.

Portia has been asked to do so many poses in so many outfits with so many hairstyle changes. I don't know how she manages to keep smiling. Maybe her face is stuck in that position. Looks painful if you ask me.

Our class would be at the aquarium by now. They're probably having lots of fun.

I'm bored with all the waiting around and I

have already scoffed the crackers and bananas. The photographer said lunch would be delivered soon. Apparently it's gourmet sandwiches. I'm hoping they're on white bread. Mom never lets us eat white bread because she says it contains toxic bleaches that rot your stomach.

Except for the free food, I still don't know what Portia sees in this modeling.

Tuesday, March 30, 6:45 p.m.

My bedroom.

Well, the photo shoot is finally over. It took us all day. First, we had the indoor shots, then the outdoor shots. Then we redid some indoor shots because they didn't come out properly the first time. GRRRR!!!

The photographer said the photos would go straight to the advertising company and the brochure would be printed and delivered in the next few days. It all sounds so quick!

The photographer also told Portia she was a "natural" and, of course, Portia believed her. The way things are going, we'll need wider doorways at home so my sister can fit her big head through them.

Mom got home just after we did. She said she had a massive day, flying to Mr. Maximus's office, running the workshop and then flying back, but everything went well and everyone seemed happy (as you'd hope at a LAUGHTER workshop).

When I asked Mom what was for dinner, she said she was too tired to cook. She asked me if I could put something together, so leftover lentil salad it was. I didn't mind helping out and I wasn't that hungry anyway because of all the gourmet sandwiches I ate earlier. They were free, after all, and yummy, and on white bread.

I wonder if that's why I have a stomachache now? Six sandwiches is a lot.

Wednesday, March 31, 7:22 p.m.

Sitting at my desk.

When I asked Caitlin and Jolie how the excursion went, they said it was *FABULOUS*. They even saw baby manatees. Can you believe it? I've always wanted to see a manatee in real life, but instead I got to spend the day watching Portia get her photo taken. Somehow, it's not the same.

When Caitlin and Jolie told Portia about the baby manatees, she wasn't listening properly and mumbled something about dolphins being really intelligent. Then she went back to the magazine she was reading (the one Mr. Divine gave her). She had it opened to a page listing the latest fashion tips. She's sooooo *OBSESSED!*

Jolie told us she's picking up her kitten from

Flynn this afternoon. When she asked if we wanted to come, Caitlin and I said yes. We still have to ask our moms but they won't mind. Portia said she didn't want to come because she had more important things to do.

"Like what?" asked Caitlin.

"Model things," Portia replied.

Caitlin looked rather peeved at that. I tried telling her she needn't worry, that cats just weren't Portia's thing, but she said it wasn't what Portia had said but the way she said it.

After school I came home and asked Mom if it was okay if I went over to Flynn's with Caitlin and Jolie. She said yes, rather distractedly. Or maybe I should say *ABSTRACTEDLY*, because she was doing one of her abstract paintings that had thick strokes and tiny dots in one corner, and nothing much else.

I rode my scooter over to Jolie's, where she and Caitlin were waiting for me. When we got to Flynn's, he was out the back playing with the kittens.

"Hi," he said. "Where's your twin? I thought you did everything together."

Luckily, Jolie stopped me from saying anything by squeezing my arm. Sometimes I get sick of silly twin comments.

Anyway, back to the kittens: one was orange, one was gray, and one was white with black and

tan and orange patches (tortoiseshell, Flynn called it).

Jolie picked up the tortoiseshell kitten and said that was the one she wanted. She said she was going to call him Jester because it was April Fools' Day tomorrow. The name suits him because he's quite cheeky.

When I got home, Mom was still locked in her studio, which sounds fancy but it's really just the end section of our creaky old porch. Portia was in our room trying on outfits. Her clothes were strewn everywhere, even on my side of the room. GRRRR!!!

We have an out-of-uniform day at school on Friday, so she's already worrying about what to wear. When I told her it didn't matter, that shorts and a T-shirt would do, she looked at me like I was an alien.

"Of course it matters, darling," she said. "Now I'm a model people will be taking extra notice of me. Personal appearance is so important in my business."

Oh, please!

I stalked out to look for Mom. It was the second night in a row that she hadn't prepared any dinner. Cheese and lettuce sandwiches tonight: my specialty.

Thursday, April 1, 8:08 a.m.

April Fools' Day!

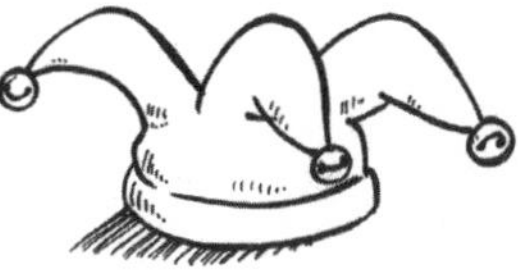

Today is April Fools' Day, but Portia's drive to become a famous model is no longer a joke. The mall brochures arrived in our mailbox this morning and she's in them, looking super-stylish and super-sophisticated.

For only the second time in her life, Portia bounced out of bed at six o'clock, this time to check the mailbox. When I heard a bloodcurdling scream (from my bed, where I was trying to go back to sleep after being woken by bouncy Portia), I thought something horrible had happened, but I soon realized it was a scream of joy not terror. Phew!

The next thing I knew, Portia was jumping up

and down on my bed shouting, “It’s here! It’s here!” As if I couldn’t guess.

Rubbing sleep from my eyes, I tried to focus on the pages Portia was shoving at me. At the same time, Mom stumbled in to ask what was going on. Portia snatched the brochure off me and thrust it at Mom. We gathered round and peered at the photos. Portia was in six shots over several pages. My sister, the model!

Mom made us a celebratory breakfast of pancakes and maple syrup. She even gave us a dollop each of ice cream (organic and low-fat, of course). It was the best breakfast ever.

Portia said that because she only had one brochure, she was going to nick some extra copies from the other mailboxes in the street. Mom shot her a stern look and I thought she was going to tell her off, but she just said, "Make sure you don't get caught. And take your sister with you."

So, once again, I was roped into helping Portia. It's the story of my life. We scurried down the street in our pajamas and slippers raiding mailboxes before running back home, arms loaded with brochures and giggling all the way.

Oops! I just saw the time. I must get ready for school. Wish I could have pancakes for breakfast every morning.

Thursday, April 1, 7:51 p.m.

Killing time...

Portia and I are holed up in our bedroom—yet again—while Mom fills the house with the scent of musk incense and her meditation students fill it with "ommms." Hopefully the agony will be over soon so we can reclaim our living room to watch *River's Town.*

Most surprisingly, Mr. Maximus—The Silver Man—is doing the meditation class too. Mom is his "flavor-of-the-month," as Gran would say. I hope it's all *INNOCENT* and Mom has told him about her "friendship" with Mr. Divine, otherwise things could get complicated.

As for Portia, she's now a *MAJOR CELEBRITY* at school. All day she was showing off the

mall catalog to teachers and kids, or they were coming up to her, having seen it already. One younger kid even asked for her autograph! Can you believe it?

It was impossible to speak to her all day. Hayley and Charlotte were constantly hanging around, and a girl in grade six, Cleo Rasmussen, was acting like she was Portia's new best friend.

Cleo, *BTW*, is one of the coolest girls in school. She's in the popular group, is vice-captain, sings in the choir, plays in the band, and is a brilliant runner at school carnivals. She's what Gran would call a "general all-rounder."

When Portia and I were standing in line at the canteen, Cleo sidled up to Portia and asked, "So,

Persephone, how long have you been modeling?"

Portia sent me a SECRET SIGNAL of "Here we go again," which Cleo didn't see. Then she politely told Cleo her name was Portia (more politely than I would have anyway). Cleo asked which one of us was the model and, of course, Portia made it clear very quickly that it was her. Then she asked Cleo if she had seen the latest mall catalog.

Cleo said she had and that she also saw Portia in the fashion parade. Cleo said she'd always wanted to be a model too. She was being so sickly sweet and even asked Portia if she wanted to sit with her group. Unheard of!

Portia glanced at me, then over at Caitlin and Jolie who were waiting for us at our table. "I don't know," she said. "I usually sit with my friends."

"That's fine," Cleo shrugged. "If you want to sit with little kids that's up to you, but if you change your mind you can come and sit with me and my cool friends instead."

I thought that was SUPER RUDE, but I didn't say anything because I was sure Portia would tell Cleo where to go.

Portia, however, was chewing her lip like she was seriously considering the option to ditch her friends (and me!) to sit with Cleo.

"Geez, Portia!" Cleo said. "I'm not asking you to marry me."

That's when Portia GUSHED that she would sit with them. I nearly choked. I couldn't believe my own sister was passing me over for cool Cleo. Well, maybe I could, but I didn't have to like it.

Portia paid for her fruit drink, then wandered

off with Cleo. When I got back to my gang, I told them Portia was helping Cleo with something. I couldn't tell them the truth. Caitlin was already cross with Portia and I didn't want to cause any more trouble.

Thursday, April 1, 9:38 p.m.

In my bedroom.

We've just finished watching *River's Town*. It was the best episode ever! It was so dramatic and when the show finished on a cliff-hanger, Portia and I were almost gnawing our fingernails off with the suspense. I wonder what's going to happen next week???

Friday, April 2, 7:52 a.m.

Bathroom.

I'm writing with one hand, while using toilet paper to dab my damp eyes with the other. Portia started hassling me early this morning. Out-of-uniform day is meant to be fun and uncomplicated, but Portia has made it a *MAJOR DRAMA*.

She didn't like what I was wearing, which was a striped shirt and purple shorts. I thought it looked okay, but Portia said it made me look like a walking *FASHION FAUX PAS* (I had to ask her to spell it).

What would she know? Just because she's becoming more famous every day doesn't mean she can be horrible to me. I like my clothes. I don't care what she thinks. When I told her that, she looked at me like she felt sorry for me. Which only made me angrier. Then she offered to give me a style makeover. Angrier still!

"No thanks," I told her. "Lace and satin wouldn't look any good on an archaeological dig. Besides, I prefer shorts because they're far more comfortable than the clothes you get around in."

BTW, Portia took forever in the bathroom this morning. You'd think she was preparing for one of her fashion parades, not going to school. When I groaned at her about it, she said, "Darling, a person doesn't wake up beautiful. It takes loads of hard work."

I don't think Portia is particularly beautiful at the moment. Fame has made her *UGLY*.

While I'm wearing my fashion faux pas, she's

wearing the outfit she got from *Sadie's Funky Fashion Boutique*. It's a shimmery, aqua dress, which is totally over-the-top for school. It's more like something you'd wear on a special occasion, like to a wedding.

Mom caught Portia trying on her high heels earlier and totally freaked out. She said Portia was far too young to wear heels and that she would never be allowed to wear them to school, even if she was older.

Portia argued that her foot very nearly, almost fit into Mom's shoe. Mom has small and slender

feet like Gran, while Portia and I take after Dad because our feet are *WHOPPINGLY* huge. Luckily our feet aren't hairy like his though. Well, mine aren't, but Portia's are (tee-hee).

Trying to be funny, Portia said, "If the shoe fits, I should be able to wear it."

"Ha, ha. No chance," said Mom. And that was that.

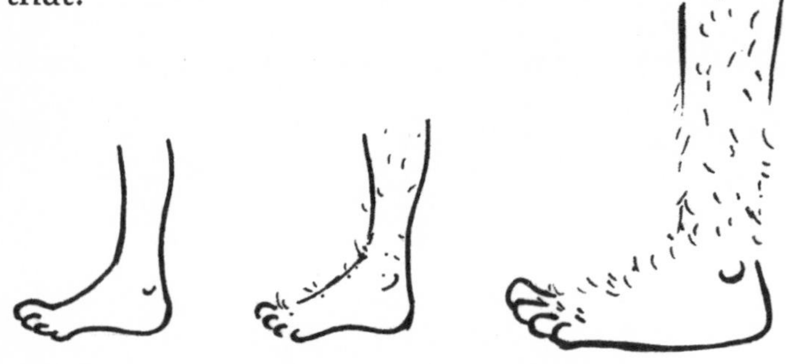

Friday, April 2, 1:07 p.m.

Sitting in a cubicle in the girls' restroom at school.

I don't make a habit of locking myself in the girls' restroom (except sometimes when I need peace and quiet or when I'm upset about having to audition for musicals—see Diary Number One), but today is an exception.

It's a good thing I brought my diary to school because it means I can vent here rather than causing a scene by telling Portia what I think of her. I don't like involving everyone else in our *TWIN TUSSLES*.

Portia has gone too far this time. All because of that snobby Cleo who thinks she's better than everyone else since she's twelve already

and in the year above us. I don't know why she's hanging around Portia. It can't be for nice reasons because I don't think Cleo is capable of being nice. Not after what I heard her say.

To rewind, while we were eating lunch, Cleo sauntered over and demanded Portia sit with her. She said Bridie had brought this cool necklace in to show everyone and she especially wanted to know what Portia thought of it. Beats me why.

Portia got all excited and went, "Oh, wow!" and let Cleo drag her away. When I walked past them on my way to the canteen, I overheard Cleo say she couldn't believe Portia and I were twins because Portia was so much cooler than me and I had absolutely no style whatsoever. She also said that if Portia and I didn't look so much alike she'd swear we weren't even related.

(Looks like she didn't like my outfit either.)

My face was burning as I slowed down to hear what Portia would say. At first, Portia tried to stick up for me, but Cleo went on and on about it until Portia flicked her hair and agreed with her, saying that she'd always had more fashion sense than me and she supposed it was just one of those things.

That's when I stormed over to my bag, grabbed my diary, and bolted in here to write this all down. Luckily for Portia I'm such a controlled person otherwise she'd have a very sore pinched arm by now. (Don't mind the smudges on the page, they're just my tears.)

When we got home, I asked Portia why she said what she did about me at lunch and she acted all confused like she couldn't even remember. Can you believe it?

When I took the time to remind her, she shrugged and said it wasn't like she'd lied because she did have better fashion sense than me, but that she didn't mean anything by it.

I think she did mean something by it though. I think she was trying to impress Cleo—at my expense. I tried telling her as much, but no matter what I said I couldn't make her see it my way. So frustrating!

Friday, April 2, 7:23 p.m.

At my desk.

You're never going to believe what's happened. Portia is so lucky! Tonight, when we were eating scrambled eggs for dinner, the phone rang. Portia answered the phone and straightaway I knew it was her agent because her voice got all serious and professional. Also, she said, "Oh, hi Hilary."

After listening for a while, Portia said, "Wow! That's awesome!" and she did a little dance on the spot. Then she handed Mom the phone. (Mom had skipped her art class with Mr. Divine because she said she was too tired: which is so unlike her.) While Mom was talking, I was dying to ask Portia what was happening, but I didn't

want to give her the satisfaction of knowing I was curious.

Mom was all smiles as she hung up and by now I was *ITCHING* to know what was going on. Thankfully, Mom put me out of my misery by blurting out, "Portia's going to be on TV!"

Completely shocked, I couldn't help but ask what for and Mom said it was for an eco-ad for a local nature reserve. When I asked what an eco-ad was, Portia said, "Oh, get with it, darling. Save water. Save trees. Save the planet. An eco-

ad. That's what we call them in the business."

I had a few ideas about what Portia could do with her "darlings" by now, but I kept tight-lipped. It wouldn't have done any good complaining anyway because Mom was busy hugging Portia and calling her a *SUPERSTAR*. Blurh!

Portia grinned at me and said that wasn't even the best part.

"What's the best part?" I sighed.

"'I'm going to be in the ad with none other than Taylor North!" she squealed.

Of course, I thought she was joking. Turns out she wasn't.

Part of me was *ECSTATIC* for Portia. Even though she'd been mean to me, deep down I was proud of her. But another part of me, that was deeper down than the proud part of me, was so

jealous. Taylor North was my favorite star, but it was my sister, my twin, who had been given the chance to meet her and work with her.

I couldn't help wondering when something good was going to happen in my life. Also, why did Portia's success make me feel so miserable? Because I knew it was wrong to feel like that, I decided to do some *ACTING* and pretend I was happy for Portia—so I didn't "rain on her parade," as Gran would say.

I forced myself to smile as I asked Portia when filming was scheduled for. She said it was next Saturday and that a limo was being sent to

pick her and Mom up at six in the morning.

A limo? It just keeps getting better for Portia!

Then Mom checked her diary and discovered that she had booked a special laughter therapy session for Mr. Maximus. It was something she couldn't get out of and she didn't want to let him down. That's when Portia looked at me.

"Perse, you'll have to come with me then," she insisted.

"I would feel better knowing you're with Portia," Mom said. "I'm sure you will be safe with the driver and the other adults on set."

Then both Portia and Mom stared at me with pleading eyes.

"But it's Caitlin's birthday party next Saturday," I reminded Portia. "Surely you're not thinking of missing it."

Portia looked guilty for a millisecond, then

shrugged and said she was working with Taylor North and that Caitlin would understand. I wasn't so sure, but Portia was adamant. When I asked who was going to tell Caitlin, Portia laughed and said not to worry, that she would explain everything to her. Which is precisely what I'm afraid of.

At lunch today, Portia told Caitlin we couldn't come to her party and Caitlin was not happy. It probably would have been better if Portia hadn't blurted out in one big rush about the television commercial and Taylor North and Mom not being able to come, and me going instead. My sister, the sledgehammer!

Caitlin asked whether Portia could do it some other day and Portia got all *HUFFY*.

"Of course I can't do it another day," she said. "I have to take the work when it comes. If you understood anything about the modeling-slash-acting business you would know that."

"I'm sorry I'm so out of the loop!" Caitlin shot

back at her. "I don't know how things work for *MAJOR CELEBRITIES* because I'm only an ordinary little person who is having an ordinary little birthday party which no one seems to care about anymore."

I tried telling Caitlin I did care, but she wasn't listening because she was sniffling loudly and looking hurt. Before any of us could stop her, she shuffled away.

"Great going, you two," Jolie said, before running after Caitlin.

I was mortified that we had just hurt our best

friend's feelings. When I asked Portia what we should do, she said, "Nothing. We should just let Caitlin get over it."

I said I didn't think Caitlin would ever get over it, but Portia said fame always came at a cost. I glared at her for causing all this fuss and for being so selfish, but she didn't notice because she was too busy admiring her fingernails.

Tuesday. April 6. 5:22 p.m.

In the living room.

Portia has locked me out of our bedroom so she can rehearse her lines for the ad she's shooting on Saturday. She's driving me nuts!

When I told Mom about it, she waved me away and told me to stop complaining. She was in her studio at the time but she wasn't painting. She was working on a report for Mr. Maximus.

I hadn't seen her paint for a few days and when I mentioned it, she said bills needed to be paid and doing work for Mr. Maximus was one way she could pay lots of bills at once. When I asked her if she enjoyed the work, she said she did and that while it wasn't quite like painting, it was still satisfying.

I also asked her whether she'd spoken to Mr. Divine lately. She said he had phoned earlier and she told him she couldn't come to class for a while, and he was fine with it. Guess I'll have to take her word for it.

Anyway, at school today Portia spent more time with Cleo. It actually made it easier because things between Portia and Caitlin are rather ICY at the moment.

I overheard Portia tell Cleo about her job with Taylor North. I'm sure Cleo nearly fainted. I swear she's obsessed with CELEBRITY-DOM. I even heard Cleo tell Portia she simply had to get Taylor North's autograph for her OR ELSE. Portia said she would try and Cleo curled her lip and sneered, "You'd better. Otherwise people might think you're not cool anymore."

That's when I realized how things are between

Cleo and Portia. Portia's trying so hard to please Cleo, but I'm not sure she'll ever succeed. I'm still angry at Portia for saying horrible things about me, but in a way I feel sorry for her too.

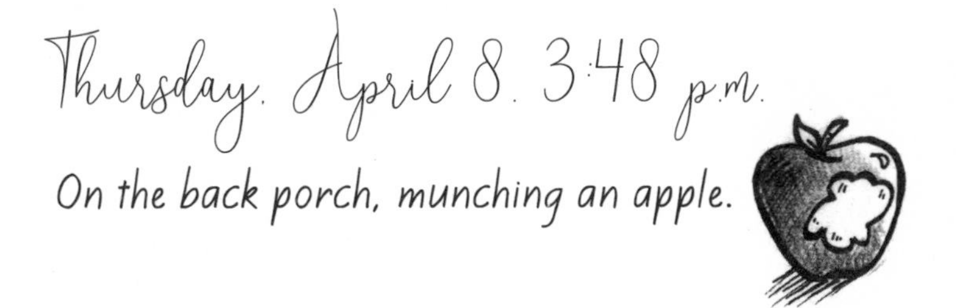

I had to rush home so I could write that I beat Portia in a geography test today! That's the second time I've beaten her. Portia's mind simply isn't on her schoolwork at the moment (Mr. Cleaver said so too) because she's so preoccupied with this modeling stuff. So I guess I have an unfair advantage, but I don't care because it's a *RARE EVENT* for me to beat Portia in anything.

Except history.

Especially if it's about Ancient Egypt.

Which I'm an expert in.

Mr. Divine and Mom are in the living room talking. I'm in the kitchen listening in on their conversation. Portia's still at ballet, so I must make sure I get this all down and fill her in later. If she behaves herself, that is.

Okay, tuning into the conversation now:

Mr. D: "I haven't seen you in class for a while, Skye. Is everything all right?"

Mom: "Everything's fine, Will. I've just been flat-out working for Morcum."

Mr. D: "Morcum?"

Mom: "You know, Morcum Maximus. He's a client, a very valuable client. Plus, he's joined my new Thursday meditation class."

Mr. D: "You didn't tell me that."

Mom: "I didn't realize I had to."

A sigh from Mr. Divine. Pacing. Then, "I thought we had something, Skye. I thought... oh, I don't know what I thought."

Mom: "We do have something. I'm busy, that's all. It doesn't mean I don't care about you."

Mr. D: "You mean that?"

Mom: "Of course!"

Now everything has gone silent. I have a feeling Mom and Mr. Divine are kissing, but I'm too chicken to peek around the corner to find out for sure.

Hang on, Mom's cell phone is ringing.

Mom: "Hello, Morcum. How are you? No, that's okay, you're not interrupting anything."

Oh! The front door just slammed, which I'm guessing was Mr. Divine leaving.

Adults can be weird sometimes.

Friday, April 9, 8:22 p.m.

In bed, under the covers and writing by flashlight.

Because we have to get up so early in the morning, Portia has placed a self-imposed curfew on us and sent us to bed early. She says she needs plenty of beauty sleep so she doesn't have panda eyes tomorrow.

I hate to tell her, but it's too late, her eyes are already panda-ish. She's been rehearsing her lines until all hours, pacing up and down the hallway with a book on her head and practicing her facial expressions in front of the mirror. She's also been tossing and turning all night, too hyped-up to sleep (and keeping me awake, I might add). I am so sick of this Portia-induced *MODEL MANIA!*

Anyway, the alarm is set for five and if I don't get some sleep I'm going to be totally useless in the morning. *TTYL.*

Saturday, April 10, 6:47 a.m.

In the limo!

I now know what a sunrise looks like, and while it is beautiful I still wish I didn't have to witness it this morning. YAWN!

Mom got up early with us and made breakfast. Boiled eggs—slightly runny—with toast soldiers to dip in them. Portia said she had too many butterflies in her stomach to fit runny eggs in there too, so I ate hers for her.

As we finished breakfast (or I should say as I finished breakfast) the doorbell rang. It was our driver, standing there in a suit and a funny chauffeur's hat. Outside, the black limo (complete with tinted windows) waited, its tailpipe frothing clouds of smoke into the cool

morning air.

Mom bustled us out the door, then took some photos as we stepped into the limo. I think I caught the driver rolling his eyes at us being totally uncool and new to the getting-into-the-limo routine, but he didn't say anything. He just silently held the door open with his white-gloved hands.

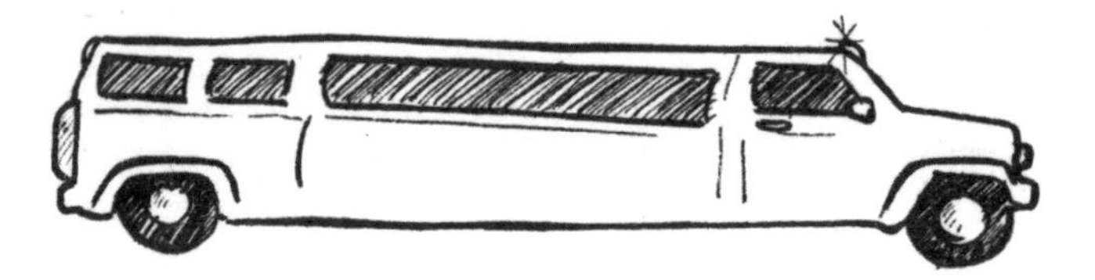

Portia and I slid onto the back seat.

"Sure beats the hatchback," Portia said, eyeing the leather seats.

I leaned back, thinking this was super-luxurious and definitely fun, but also feeling sad because we were going to miss Caitlin's party.

As if reading my thoughts, Portia said, "Don't worry, we'll make it up to her."

I nodded. Portia went quiet after that and just stared out the window. After a while she fell asleep.

Boy, I hope everything goes okay. Portia's given up a lot to be here today.

So have I.

Saturday, April 10, 11:09 a.m.

"On location" at the nature reserve.

When we arrived, the director briskly introduced himself (his name is Pearce Dragonfire), then barked out instructions to Portia about getting over to "wardrobe" and "makeup" so we could start shooting the moment Taylor North arrived. But it's been three hours and Taylor still isn't here!

The director keeps yelling, "Where is she?" to no one in particular, as he checks his watch.

Portia has had her hair and makeup done and is dressed in a khaki shirt and shorts. She looks like an *UNGLAMOROUS* and rather *PASTY* park ranger. Khaki is definitely not her color. I guess

guess that means it's not mine either.

I can tell Portia's bored. She's picking her fingernails. Every so often she goes to flick her hair, but the hairdresser keeps pulling her hand away and telling her to stop fiddling because she'll destroy all her hard work. Portia isn't the only one who's bored. I am too (only my diary is saving me from a complete brain-numbing) and the entire crew is moping around waiting for Taylor North to arrive.

Portia just asked me to play tic-tac-toe. Sure, I can do that—while I fight off about a zillion mosquitoes at the same time. TTYL.

Saturday, April 10, 11:28 a.m.

Still "on location."

Taylor North has finally arrived! Everyone sprang into action the minute she got here. Because we're so far out in the wilderness we heard the car coming from miles away. Dust swirled as a white limousine pulled up. A door opened and Taylor North, wearing black boots, black jeans, a black T-shirt, and a white denim jacket stepped out.

Instantly, Pearce Dragonfire and his attendants descended on the starlet, swooping her into embraces, and welcoming her with glittering smiles: nothing like the scowls dominating their dials moments before. No mention was made of how late she was, *BTW*.

As Portia and I stood in the background watching, a woman slightly older than Mom oozed elegantly out of the limo. She was wearing an emerald dress and high heels, which were completely out of place in a nature reserve, but which even I thought looked STUNNING.

The woman in the emerald dress began barking orders at everyone, including the director.

"We need water right now," she said. "And chairs over there in the shade."

Assistants ran left and right, following her instructions.

"No, no, no!" the woman shouted. "Over there, not there!"

Portia told me the woman was Taylor's mom. Apparently, she'd seen her before in a magazine.

Pearce Dragonfire said something to Taylor. She blew a pink bubble with her chewing gum until it burst with a *TOCK!* Then she sucked it back into her mouth, saluted Pearce and marched over to costumes where she's now getting ready.

Saturday, April 10, 11:58 a.m.

Still "on location."

Caitlin's party is due to start in two minutes. I wish I was there.

Still waiting for TN to get ready.

Saturday, April 10, 12:22 p.m.

Finally, filming has begun.

Before they went on set together, Portia and Taylor were properly introduced. It was so embarrassing watching Portia gush all over her like a burst water pipe. She said how great it was to meet her and that she'd watched every episode of *River's Town* since it started. Exactly what I'd been rehearsing to say to her all week!

Taylor didn't seem at all impressed and snorted at Portia that she should get out more. In between slapping at mosquitoes (they're everywhere out here and I'm getting eaten alive), Portia told Taylor she thought she was a terrific actress and she admired the way she stood up to Liberty when she was bullying her at school.

Taylor did a major eye roll and said loudly so *EVERYONE* could hear that she was only acting at the time and that whatever she did or said on camera was what she was told to do.

"It's just a show, dummy. None of it is real," she said with a nasty sneer.

I caught Portia's eye and sent her a *SECRET SIGNAL* of "Never mind." She nodded and pretended she didn't care, but I could tell she was crushed because she started to *MOPE*.

Now the girls are being made to stand near a creek while they recite their lines. It's wet and muddy on the creek bank and the ground is slippery and uneven. Silly place to shoot an ad if you ask me, but I'm no director.

Saturday, April 10, 2:28 p.m.

The filming fiasco continues...

Portia and Taylor were made to run through their lines about fifty times. Taylor smiled so sweetly and was so nice to Portia while the camera was on that if I hadn't already written down how rude she was earlier I'd have sworn I imagined it.

When they had a break, Taylor's smile vanished and her scowl returned. That didn't stop Portia from trying to speak to her again though.

"You must really care about the environment to be working on this campaign," she told Taylor.

All Taylor did was screw up her nose and say it didn't bother her either way and that she was only doing it for the money.

Then I heard Portia ask whether she could get Taylor's autograph because she had a friend at school who really wanted it. I thought she was asking for Cleo and I couldn't believe it, but Taylor just glared at Portia and told her to stop bothering her.

Portia is not one to take no for an answer. She told Taylor she'd skipped her friend's birthday party (at this point I realized she'd been talking about Caitlin, not Cleo) so she could meet her and that if she had her autograph it would make her friend (Caitlin) feel a whole lot better. Taylor still said no and Portia, who was getting a little red and *FLUSTERED*, said surely it wouldn't hurt her to write her name on a piece of paper for her.

"What's the big deal?" Portia added.

But Taylor wasn't listening; she was peering at the bushes behind her, with a rather scared look on her face.

"What's that noise?" she said.

Even I heard the rustling from where I was standing behind the crew. It sounded like something was crawling through the undergrowth. When a reptilian head poked through the bushes, Taylor totally lost it, screaming, "Snake! Snake!"

The film crew shouted and jostled each other, trying to get out of the way. In her rush to escape, Taylor knocked Portia flying, sending her squealing and sliding down the slippery creek bank where she landed with a SPLASH! in the water. I could see Portia was totally soaked and totally fuming.

I tried telling everyone that it was only a lizard and not a snake, but no one was listening and by then it was too late anyway.

Now Portia's sitting in a chair nearby, getting her ankle iced because she twisted it when she fell in the creek. She's pretty tough, though, and isn't even crying. I think she's too angry for that.

Pearce Dragonfire is tearing his hair out and shouting, "What are we going to do now? We haven't finished shooting yet and this kid can't even stand up!"

What a disaster.

Uh oh! I just noticed everyone looking at me. Can't imagine why...

Saturday, April 10, 4:21 p.m.

Sitting in the limousine,
leaving the nature reserve.

To say I was dragged kicking and screaming to "wardrobe" and "makeup" is an exaggeration, but only a teeny-tiny one.

With Portia out of action due to her twisted ankle, she wasn't in any state to finish filming. That's what everyone, including Portia, told me. But I didn't think that meant I had to finish the task for her. Unfortunately, I couldn't convince Pearce Dragonfire that I wasn't the girl for the job. So, with no way out, I was dressed in clean khaki, made to stand next to the ODIOUS Taylor North and told to recite the lines Portia was meant to say.

I was totally terrified of getting in front of the camera! More than that, I was totally terrified of going anywhere near Taylor North. I'd seen how nasty she was to Portia and I was sure she was going to be nasty to me too.

Luckily, although Taylor's mom is *ULTRA-GLAMOROUS* and likes ordering people about, she apparently has manners because she made Taylor apologize to Portia. Frankly, I think Taylor would rather have bitten off her own tongue, but she did apologize. Mrs North also told Taylor to give Portia an autographed photo of her, but Portia said politely that she didn't want one anymore, thanks all the same.

I whizzed through my lines to get the filming over *ASAP* so we could head home. When Portia and I finally climbed into the limo, we were both so relieved. We're totally covered in mosquito

bites, *BTW*. I can't wait to have a shower and rub some of Mom's soothing aloe vera ointment on my red welts.

I told Portia I was sorry things didn't work out with Taylor. Naturally, she was upset, but I'm happy to say my sister is a *TROUPER*. She even thanked me for standing in for her even though I didn't want to and was clearly terrified.

Now she's sound asleep. It's funny watching her snore with her mouth open wide, but she's worked hard lately so I'll let her be. I might even have a nap myself.

Portia and I tried calling Caitlin when we got home but there was no answer. Maybe they went out for dinner. Maybe she was screening our call. Who knows, but we left a message anyway.

Mom made us Thai fish cakes and vegetarian stir-fry noodles for dinner. Delicious. We told her all about the day and how horrible Taylor North had been. She sat and listened to everything. At the end of it all she told us how proud she was.

Portia was silent for a while, then blurted out, "What if I don't want to be a model anymore?"

I was so shocked I stopped eating—midway

through a mouthful! Mom laughed and told Portia it was up to her, which made Portia look relieved.

"Modeling isn't what I thought it would be," she said sadly. "It was fun for a while, but I'm totally over it now because it's too hard and I miss doing things with my friends and I'm tired all the time and Perse beats me in tests, and I simply can't bear that."

So, I guess Portia's modeling career is officially over.

Sunday, April 11, 12:09 p.m.

At my desk.

Arrggh, I am still scratching like crazy from all the mosquito bites. We both are. Poor Portia's face is covered in red lumps. She even has one on the end of her nose. It's very unattractive. Her twisted ankle is slightly better. It's still bandaged, but she's hobbling bravely around trying not to let it get her down.

We just got back from Caitlin's. Portia and I went over to take her present to her. When we rang Caitlin's doorbell who should answer but Jolie! Apparently they'd had a sleepover. Jolie was surprised and happy to see us. She made a joke that there was a famous girl on the

doorstep, then peered at Portia's face and asked what happened.

Portia explained about the mosquitoes as she scratched her neck, then her elbow. Caitlin appeared in the hallway, her hair still wet from the shower. She was wearing a fluffy white bathrobe and white rabbit slippers that looked brand new. Apparently, they were birthday presents from her parents.

I spoke first. "We came to wish you happy birthday—."

"And to give you this," Portia finished for me.

Caitlin was obviously still mad and upset with us because she reluctantly took the box Portia handed her and said we didn't have to get her anything. Then Jolie herded us into the kitchen where Caitlin's parents were. Mrs. Marciano was fixing a clock with a screwdriver and Mr. Marciano was reading the newspaper.

"How did the filming go?" Mrs. Marciano asked.

Portia looked uncomfortable and said it wasn't so great. Then Mrs. Marciano asked about her face and her ankle and everyone wanted to know everything at once, but Portia went all quiet and didn't seem to know what to say: for once in her life.

Anyway, while Portia looked at the floor and scratched her itchy bites, I studied the angel fish in the tank on the kitchen bench and

Caitlin unwrapped her present. She held up a baby-pink satin nightie with lace trimming around the sleeves and hem. Then she said—breathlessly—that she loved it and asked us where we got it from.

Portia and I swapped a SECRET SIGNAL of "Yay!" and said we'd bought it from *Sadie's Funky Fashion Boutique.*

Then Jolie asked, "So, are you going to tell us what Taylor North is really like?"

Portia shrugged. "Actually, she's quite rude."

Immediately, Caitlin and Jolie demanded to know all the GOSS, so we spent the next fifteen minutes telling them about our "brush with fame," as Gran would say. We didn't leave anything out. Not even the part about Taylor knocking Portia in the creek and me having to stand in for her.

"After yesterday, I'm never watching *River's Town* again," Portia sighed.

Caitlin looked worried and said perhaps that was going too far. Then we all laughed because none of us were sure we could give up our favorite show: not yet anyway.

Jolie asked when the ad would be on television and Portia groaned and said she wasn't sure she ever wanted to see it. I wasn't sure either, considering half of the ad would be me. I wonder if anyone will be able to tell the difference?

Spotting the computer in the corner of the room, I saw it had a photo of Caitlin and Jolie on the screen. It was obviously taken at yesterday's party so I asked if we could have a look. We gathered round the computer and Portia clicked the mouse to move through the slide show.

There were lots of photos of Caitlin; the rollerskating rink and the cake (a GINORMOUS pink butterfly with yellow, swirly patterns); several of Caitlin and Jolie pulling faces at the camera; Charlotte and Hayley holding hands as they skated; even a photo of Flynn and the other boys falling over. When we got to a photo of Caitlin sitting alone and looking sad, she snatched the mouse and minimized the screen saying, "Show's over."

Portia brought the photo back up on screen. When she asked Caitlin why she looked so sad, Caitlin shrugged and said it was because two of her best friends weren't at her party and that she had missed us.

"Really?" Portia and I said together.

"Really," Caitlin said. "Couldn't you tell how upset I was all week?"

"Upset?" Portia said. "I thought you were just angry at me because I couldn't go and because I made Perse miss out on it too. I thought you didn't want me there after the way I treated you."

But Caitlin explained that it had been the *EXACT OPPOSITE*. She wanted us at her party so bad and she thought we didn't care about her anymore, especially Portia because she'd been spending so much time with Cleo.

"I didn't say anything," continued Caitlin,

"because I knew how much your modeling-slash-acting career meant to you. Plus, I knew how important it was that Perse supported you, being your twin sister and all."

That's when Portia admitted she realized Cleo was using her. Portia also admitted that Cleo had been badgering her into asking Hilary to be her agent too.

"She's so pushy," Portia said, shaking her head. "I can't believe I ever wanted her to like me."

Then she turned to me and—wonder of wonders—apologized for all the awful *MODEL-MANIA* things she had said and done to me lately. I was stunned and relieved and touched and I didn't know what to say, so I just gave her a tight twin hug and said it was okay.

Then Portia broke the news that she was giving up modeling because it wasn't what she

wanted anymore. Caitlin asked what it was she did want and Portia said she wanted to be a normal girl who hung out with her friends. Caitlin and Jolie both said that sounded good, then we all got a bit mushy, and maybe there were hints of tears in our eyes as we had a group hug. Things finally felt like they were getting back to normal between us.

Portia said there was one other thing she wanted, and that was a piece of butterfly cake

if there was any left. I seconded that, closely followed by Caitlin and Jolie. Then we all looked at Mrs. Marciano.

Mr. Marciano dropped his newspaper into his lap and said, "It's a little early for cake, isn't it?"

All us girls, Mrs. Marciano included, shouted, "It's never too early for cake!"

Then we all ate *COPIOUS* amounts of cake which, of course, we won't dare mention to Mom.

I've come to the end of my second diary but never fear, I'm off to the mall later to buy another one!

Before I sign off I must mention that Mr. Divine is here. We just finished lunch. Mom made fennel and artichoke salad—not one of her best creations—but at least it didn't include asparagus (my least favorite food.)

Anyway, Mom and Mr. Divine are drinking cups of ginger tea in the garden. I can see them out my window, sitting under the jacaranda tree. They're holding hands and looking very contented.

Before Mr. Divine came over, Mom said that

Gran had phoned. She's back from Barbados and mentioned to Mom that she's going to take us to Fiji for the school vacation like she promised. I can't wait!

Mom isn't coming. She wants to spend quality time with Mr. Divine because she's been so busy lately and has *NEGLECTED* him. But now she's "seen the light" and is going to make it up to him.

If I wasn't so *THRILLED* about going to Fiji, I might be wondering when she's going to spend quality time with Portia and me. However, with only one week left of school (four days actually, because then it will be Easter) it's going to be a scramble to get our passports ready in time. But I'll make sure it's done because I'm dying to go to Fiji and can't wait to fill you in on the marvelous adventures I am sure we'll have over there.

But you'll have to wait for my next diary for that! *TTYL*.

About the Author

Hi, I'm Aleesah, the author of this book.

I grew up in the country in Australia and had a lot of freedom as a nine year old. My older brother, my cousin, and I would ride our bikes and go exploring, build cubbyhouses and go-carts, and rescue injured animals and birds. When I wasn't outdoors, I was usually curled up on my bed reading. It was quite an addiction for me and I often got into trouble for "having my nose in a book." I loved coloring in and won loads of prizes for my efforts. Quite shockingly, I also loved school!

I wrote lots of stories and illustrated them with crazy stick figures. Like Perse, I kept a diary. And I can always remember desperately wishing I had an identical twin.

About the Illustrator

Hi, I'm Serena, the illustrator of this book.

I don't really look this freaky, but as an artist, I can make myself look as weird as I like, and you need to be able to laugh at yourself sometimes.

I grew up in the city of Melbourne, Australia, with an older brother who taught me how to wrestle, an older sister who always had the coolest clothes and jewelry, and a younger sister who enjoyed following me around everywhere!

I loved drawing, writing notes in my diary, dressing up our pet cat in dolls' clothes, and creating mini adventures in our huge backyard. When I was nine years old, long socks were really cool, funny dresses with lots of frills and buttons were cool, straight hair was cool, and even big teeth were cool... unfortunately, I was not cool.

Serena

Other titles in the series